HOW THE ROBIN GOT ITS
RED BREAST

A LEGEND OF THE SECHELT PEOPLE

HOW THE ROBIN GOT ITS RED BREAST
Copyright © 1993 The Sechelt Nation
Principal illustrations, based on traditional Sechelt
designs, copyright © 1993 by Charles Craigan

NIGHTWOOD EDITIONS
R.R. 22, 3692 Beach Avenue
Roberts Creek, BC Canada, V0N 2W2

Sixth Printing 2004

Printed in China
Design by Roger Handling

Canadian Cataloguing in Publication Data

Main entry under title:
  How the robin got its red breast

  ISBN 0-88971-158-5

  1. Sechelt Indians—Legends—Juvenile literature.* 2. Indians
of North America—British Columbia—Legends—Juvenile
literature. 3. Robins—Folklore—Juvenile literature. 4.
Legends—British Columbia—Juvenile literature.
I. Craigan, Charlie. II. Sechelt Nation.
E99.S21H69 1993   j398.24'528842   C93-091652-2

HOW THE ROBIN GOT ITS
RED BREAST

A LEGEND OF THE SECHELT PEOPLE
ILLUSTRATED BY CHARLIE CRAIGAN

NIGHTWOOD EDITIONS

In the very beginning when the world was young and some of the first Sechelt people were living in a cave, many things were different than they are today. One of these was the robin. There was a robin, and he loved to get up early in the morning and cheer the first people with his happy song just like robins do today, but he lacked something. He did not have that glowing red breast that nowadays lends a splash of bright colour to our green west coast spring. He was just grey and dull all over.

At the time of this story the first people needed cheering up because the weather had been bad for a long time and it was bitterly cold outside. Day after day the family crowded together in the cave—the grandfather, the grandmother, their sons and daughters, the wives and husbands of the sons and daughters, and many children and babies.

One day they realized they were running out of food to eat and wood to keep themselves warm. So the young men of the group were sent out, some to get wood and some to get meat. The old man and the women stayed in the cave with the children.

The grandfather watched the fire and kept it going. Even when the women and children went to sleep, he stayed up and tended the fire. The only wood they had left was a few handfuls of sticks and bark chips, so he had to ration it out a tiny bit at a time, but he dare not let the flames die lest the babies and little children get chilled and become ill.

The young men stayed away many days hunting and looking for wood, and all that time the old man stayed up. The women lay down near the fire, the children tucked under blankets made of cedar bark, and each time they woke up, they were relieved to see their fire still going.

Finally, all that was left were a few little embers. The grandfather kept them alive by dropping little twigs on them and blowing until the coals glowed brightly. But he was growing more tired every minute, and late in the night, he fell asleep. The embers grew dim and the cave began to cool.

Towards morning the robin came along to sing his cheery wakeup song, but when he peered into the cave he was alarmed to see the fire all but dead. He hopped into the cave past the mothers and babies and the old man, who were all deeply sleeping, and when he reached the firebed the robin began to beat his wings. A draft swept across the cool grey coals and a dusting of ashes settled over the sleeping people. The robin flapped more rapidly, and after a while the embers began to glow again, weakly at first, then with a rich red that warmed the dark cave. The bird's bulging little breast reflected the red glow of the fire, and soon the heat began to make him uncomfortable, but he kept flapping his wings so the fire would not die.

Later in the morning the little bird heard the call of the hunters coming back from their long journey. Just as they entered the cave, the bird flew out, and as he flew past them, the men noticed something they had never seen before. The breast of the robin was the colour of a glowing ember.

Even now the breast of the robin has a fiery redness which can add a spot of warmth to the cloudiest day.

About Charlie Craigan

Charles Joseph (Charlie) Craigan, who illustrated this story, was born in Sechelt BC in 1969. His natural artistic talent began showing itself while he was still a Grade Five student at Sechelt Elementary and was further developed while working with carvers Arnold Jones and Jamie Jeffries. Charlie is a member of the Sechelt Indian Band and lives on the band lands in Sechelt.

Charlie dedicates the illustrations in this book to the elders of the Sechelt nation.

The Sechelt Nation

The Sechelt Nation, a division of the Coast Salish family of first nations peoples, originally occupied the southern portion of what is now known as the Sunshine Coast, from Gower Point near Gibsons to Saltery Bay, south of Powell River. At time of European contact the Sechelt (shishalh) occupied some 80 scattered village sites, the main tribal groupings being centred around four principal villages at xenichen (at the head of Jervis Inlet), ts'unay (at Deserted Bay, Jervis Inlet), tewanek (in Sechelt Inlet) and kalpilin (Pender Harbour). A populous and peaceful people, the Sechelt enjoyed a comparatively prosperous existence owing to their benign climate and an abundance of salmon, herring, and other food resources. Estimates of original population range from 5,000 to 20,000, but by the time of the first official census in 1881, Sechelt population had plunged to a mere 167, mostly as a result of introduced diseases.

Father Paul Durieu of the Oblate missionaries converted the Sechelt to Catholicism by 1865 and founded a central mission at the present Sechelt village on Trail Bay in 1868. The modern Sechelt are one of Canada's most progressive first nations groups, having been involved in the operation of a deepsea fishing vessel, a commercial airline, a salmon hatchery, an office and cultural complex, a large gravel-mining project, and other business enterprises. In 1986 the Sechelt gained international notice when their long campaign to gain control of their own affairs culminated in the successful passage of Bill C-93, The Sechelt Indian Band Self-Government Act, making them the first band in Canada to achieve native self-government. In 1993 the Sechelt band numbered 844 members, 450 of whom lived on band lands.